THIS BOOK BELONGS TO:

SECRET IDENTITY

Do not fill this bit in or
Dr Septic will know who you are
....

SUPERHERO NAME

....

OTHER BOOKS BY MICHAEL COX

Johnny Catbiscuit to the Rescue!

Johnny Catbiscuit and the Abominable Snotmen!

Johnny Catbiscuit and the Tentacles of Doom!

Little Fred Riding Hood

JOHNNY CATBISCUIT

AND THE STOLEN SECRETS!

MICHAEL COX

ILLUSTRATED BY GARY DUNN

EGMONT

To Terry and Tom Bentley

EGMONT
We bring stories to life

Johnny Catbiscuit and the Stolen Secrets!
first published in Great Britain 2008
by Egmont UK Limited
239 Kensington High Street
London W8 6SA

Text copyright © Michael Cox 2008
Illustrations copyright © Gary Dunn 2008

The moral rights of the author and illustrator have been asserted

ISBN 978 1 4052 3739 0

1 3 5 7 9 10 8 6 4 2

A CIP catalogue record for this title is available from the British Library

Printed and bound in Great Britain by the CPI Group

CONTENTS

CHAPTER ONE
SILLY BILLY'S

As they made their way along Busyville High Street, twelve-year-old Wayne Bunn and his pet cat Felix Pawson could hardly contain their excitement. For this was a very special day. A day so special, so important and so utterly mind-boggling that, had anyone told Wayne about it twelve months earlier, he would have decided that they were stark, staring mad!

But Wayne knew that this amazing day was

for real. He and his pal would soon arrive at 'Silly Billy's!', an innocent-looking joke shop on the High Street. And then they would be taking part in a very special occasion. An occasion so remarkable and out-of-this-world that mere mortals can only dream of such things!

For Wayne Bunn and Felix Pawson were not an ordinary boy and his cat, but a pair of exceptional individuals. A pair of exceptional individuals who led a unique and astonishing secret life.

But more on that later. We must now return to the joke shop, where its owner, Silly Billy, wearing his familiar, radiant-red bowtie, bright

yellow shirt and luminous green trousers, was ushering Wayne and Felix inside.

'Welcome, gentlemen!' he said. 'And how are you on this extraordinary day?'

'Nervous!' said Wayne. 'But otherwise fine! Er, how are you, Mr Billy?'

'I'm fine, too!' said Silly Billy. 'Apart from being caught out by a prankster!'

'Well, you are a joke-shop owner!' said Wayne. 'I suppose it's to be expected.'

'Yes, you're probably right!' agreed Silly Billy. 'But I was left in a right fix!'

However, before Wayne had a chance to ask what sort of a 'fix' he'd been left in, Silly Billy

glanced at his watch, and said, 'But you don't want to be listening to my little grumbles. Or you'll be late for your special event!'

And he escorted Wayne and Felix behind his counter, where he slid aside a floor panel and opened the trapdoor concealed beneath it.

'Good luck to you both!' said Silly Billy.

Wayne and Felix slipped through the trapdoor, then clambered down a rickety ladder to a long, snaking corridor. This led them to some workshops where brainy-types in white coats stared at computer screens or fiddled with custard-squirting cameras, glow-in-the-dark chattering teeth and invisible invisible-ink.

4

Then, at the far end of those bustling workshops, Wayne typed a complicated code of hexadecimals, Roman numerals, Egyptian hieroglyphs and incoherent squiggles into the keypad of a gleaming, rocket-shaped glass lift. A rocket-shaped lift which now **WHIZZED** him

and Felix down to yet another long, snaking corridor, some stairs (to be walked down backwards) and a pair of magnificent, hand-carved, cherry-wood doors. They went through the doors into a vast, mirrored hall, lit by a thousand scented candles and filled with the most astonishing collection of human beings anyone could ever hope to meet on Space-Speck Earth.

'Sheesh!' purred Felix, gazing in wonder at the assembly of EAPs[*]. 'Awesome, or what?'

All that remained was for the two friends to slip into one of the spy-proof 'changing' rooms and undergo the transformations which would make them recognisable to their fellow guests.

* EAP: Extremely Astounding Person

Wayne was the first to 'change'. Reaching into a black bin liner, he pulled out a magnificent silver vest, on which the initials 'JC' were picked out. This was followed by a glittering golden cape, golden gloves and a pair of winged boots. Next came a silver mask. And finally, a sleek, biometric, plasma-chuffed wrist-pod. Wayne had the outfit on in seconds. Then, hands on hips, he took a deep breath, and said:

'Johnny's brave, Johnny's no fool
And Felix the cat is super cool.
So villains and cheapskates better beware,
This plucky pair just DO NOT SCARE!'

And, as he did, an astonishing change

7

overcame him. First, his entire body began to make a muffled humming noise. Then a spectral, purple light flashed and leapt around him, shimmering and throbbing eerily, whilst occasionally turning to shades of yellow and red. And finally, as the humming died away and the light faded, his whole body began to heave and ripple. Muscles bulged, sinews strengthened, flesh became iron-hard and senses razor-sharp!

The transformation was complete. Gone were the scraggy shoulders of schoolboy Wayne Bunn. Gone, too, were his bony chest, scrawny legs and sticky-out ears. No longer could he be knocked down with your little finger. Now it

would have taken a speeding express train. But even that would have come off worse.

Standing in front of Felix, silver vest pulled tight across his powerful chest, was the tall, tanned and remarkably handsome young superhero, Johnny Catbiscuit. The remarkable young superhero who, with the help of Felix Pawson, had spent the previous twelve months saving animals, children and grown-ups from all sorts of doom, disaster and danger, whilst bringing justice to wrongdoers everywhere.

Now it was time for Felix to transform. Johnny reached into the black bin liner, took out a shimmering gold and silver super-suit

9

and a pair of golden gloves and gave them to his little pal. Felix had them on in a flash.

A microsecond later, Felix's lithe body began to grow, his muscles swelling rapidly beneath his beautiful blue-grey fur. Soon he looked more like a young lion-cub than a cuddly domestic cat. Next, he rose on to his hind legs, standing almost a metre tall. And lastly, his forepaws changed into muscular hands, complete with thumbs and fingers, enabling him to pick up his sparkling outfit and have it on in a flash. Proudly admiring his splendid reflection in the changing-room mirror, Felix placed his newly-formed hands on his hips and

said, 'Right, partner! Let's strut our funky stuff!'

Ten minutes later, Johnny and Felix were sitting alongside their superhero companions in the great hall, enjoying a sumptuous banquet of roast firedrake in kumquat butter, all served up on a bed of pickled seaweed, followed by fairy cakes, three sorts of jelly and a splendid trifle.

Then, with the feast finally over, the guests sighed contentedly and sat back, and a small, silver-haired woman walked on to the laser-lit **iPOdiUM™** in front of them. Above the **iPOdiUM™** dangled a red silken banner on which the words *ONE HUNDRED AND EIGHTY-THIRD GOLDEN GOSH* AWARDS*

* GOSH: Guild of Superheroes

12

EXCLUSIVELY SPONSORED BY SUPERHERO SUPPORT SERVICE SOLUTIONS were picked out in shimmering silver satin.

Yes, it was that time of year again. The extraordinary and supremely courageous superheroes of that picturesque and pleasant land known as the Realms of Normality were gathered to celebrate yet another twelve months of triumph over all that is wicked, wayward and worthless in this world.

Or, to put it another way, triumph over that evil genius Dr Septacemius J. Septic. The same Dr Septacemius J. Septic who, aided by his mob of loathsome lackeys, devised fiendish and

cunning plots to take over the Realms of Normality and enslave its inhabitants. He longed to subject them to pain and suffering on a daily basis. Such was his wickedness!

And this had been an outstanding year in the superheroes' never-ending battle against Dr Septic, unmatched in superhero history. A year awash with achievement, which, in no small part, was due to the astonishing exploits of Johnny Catbiscuit and Felix Pawson.

In fact, it had been *such* a good year that the assembled super-crusaders were feeling exceptionally pleased with themselves. You might even go as far as to say they were aglow

14

with pride and self-satisfaction. Pride and self-satisfaction which, during the troubled days to come, some of them would bitterly regret, constantly asking themselves just how they could have become so smug and slapdash.

But back to the awards ceremony! A very important moment had been reached.

'And our next award,' announced the silver-haired woman, 'is for the Most Promising Newcomers. And to present it, we have no less a superhero than . . . Animal Protection Man!'

A small, grey-bearded man pushed his walking frame across the stage and took the envelope. As he did, everyone cheered.

Well, everyone but Johnny and Felix. They simply exchanged worried glances and shuffled nervously in their seats. For, in the next moment, they would discover whether it was they who had won that coveted award. Or, disappointment of disappointments, their rivals and friends, Vest and Pants Lad and his partner, Timmy the Human Onion.

So, it was with sweaty palms, pounding hearts and knotted tums that Johnny Catbiscuit and Felix Pawson watched Animal Protection Man fumble with the bronze envelope, tear it open, pull out a card, take a deep breath, and say . . .

CHAPTER TWO
WINNERS!

'And the Most Promising Newcomers are . . .
JOHNNY CATBISCUIT AND FELIX PAWSON!'

The hall went wild! Feet were stamped, backs slapped and glasses clinked.

'WELL DONE!' yelled Vest and Pants Lad, without the slightest hint of jealousy or ill-feeling. 'You both truly deserve it!'

Then, to even more tumultuous applause, and blushing from head to toe (or paws, in

Felix's case), the chums made their way to the stage. As they did so, an enormous 3D multi-megascreen exploded into life, displaying highlights (some of them on-the-spot video footage, and others reconstructions made using actors) from the pair's daring and triumphant exploits of the previous twelve months.

'**SPEECH! SPEECH!**' roared the assembled superheroes.

'Well, what a year it's been for me and my sidekick!' grinned Johnny, fiddling self-consciously with his magnificent silver **KERSPLATT!** trophy. 'And it seems like only five minutes since that remarkable day when I

18

met Animal Protection Man. That amazing day which changed my life forever!'

Johnny and Animal Protection Man swapped affectionate grins. 'I must also say,' continued Johnny, 'that without the inspiration provided

by **TIME-SLIP SANDRA**, THE SILVER RIPPLE, **DANGER DUDE**, **BODACIOUS BABE**, CAPTAIN UNSTOPPABLE and many, many more of our superhero colleagues, I and my brave sidekick Felix Pawson could not have pulled off a fraction of the amazing victories we've achieved this year.'

Johnny placed an affection-ate arm around his trusty side-kick's shoulders.

'SPEECH! SPEECH!' cried

20

a dozen superheroes, pointing at Felix.

'Thank you! Thank you!' said Felix, holding up his own (somewhat smaller) KerSPLaTT! trophy. 'I really don't deserve it!' Then he paused, raised his eyebrows mischievously, and said, 'But then again . . . maybe I do!'

This brought roars of laughter from all the superheroes.

'But seriously, folks, this is so cool!' continued Felix, once more raising his trophy. Then he pointed at Johnny and said, 'And this guy . . . is even cooler!'

More cheers and stamping followed as Johnny grinned and said, 'And, of course, we

21

must also thank Jatinder and all her colleagues at Superhero Support Service Solutions for their incredibly useful advice and information.'

'**TO JATINDER AND SSSS!**' roared the delighted audience. 'Where would we be without them?'

'And last, but not least,' continued Johnny, 'I must pass on my heartfelt thanks to my gran who, for security reasons, not to mention the demands of an extremely busy home-baking schedule, cannot be here today.'

This brought nods of approval and another round of applause.

Then Johnny and Felix returned to their

seats, clutching their awards and grinning from ear to ear.

The woman signalled for quiet. 'And finally!' she announced. 'We come to the most eagerly anticipated moment of the evening – **THE SUPERHERO OF THE YEAR AWARD!** And to present the golden **WHOOSH!**, we have the winner of last year's Superhero of the Year Award – the fearless, the awesome and the utterly invincible . . . *CAPTAIN UNSTOPPABLE!*

Again the hall erupted into applause. But then, as Captain Unstoppable reached into the golden envelope, an expectant hush fell over the entire room.

23

'For his valiant defeat of that loathsome trickster Gluey Hughie and his vile plan to cover the highways and byways of our lovely country with industrial-strength super-gloo. The winner is . . . **THE SILVER RIPPLE!**'

Roars and cheers followed as the audience watched a brief viddy-clip of the Silver Ripple scrunching himself up into a supercharged, silver golf ball and flying at Dr Septic's mischievous, but gormless, gloo-squirting stepson Gluey Hughie, leaving him comatose in less than a nanosecond.

The Silver Ripple now gave an acceptance speech. The only thing that slightly spoiled this

24

wonderful moment was when he dropped his fabulous solid gold **WHOOSH!** trophy. But he made a joke about having 'had his fingers nibbled by a small boy'. This meant nothing to

the other superheroes, but they all laughed.

Then, as the Ripple returned to his seat, the Guild of Superheroes emblem appeared on the megascreen.

It was time to close the ceremony with the Superhero Anthem. Everyone pushed back their seats and stood up, clearing their throats.

But, before the trio of saxophonists (all retired superheroes) could strike up the anthem, the silver-haired woman came back on to the stage and said, 'Fellow superheroes, before we begin our glorious tribute to all that is good, decent and heroic, I have a surprise for you. As you know, our esteemed

super-colleague Hillman Avenger cannot be with us tonight, as he is busy with urgent, heroic business in the Southern Semisphere. Nevertheless, by the miracle of satellite-enabled, 3D, hologrammatical, avatar-inducing laser-link, Hillman will lead us in our singing of the Superhero Anthem.'

Then she snapped her fingers and cried, 'Take it away, Hillman!'

But now something unexpected happened. Something so shocking and disturbing that the assembled superheroes all took two paces back and let out a gasp of disbelief. Because, instead of the likeness of Hillman Avenger, another 3D

image materialised on the **iPOdiUM**™. An image so detested by the assembled examples of goodness, virtue and courage that some of the more impulsive ones actually began hissing and jeering in a most undignified way.

But, in the circumstances, they could have been excused. For, staring down at them, his icy eyes aglitter with malice and evil, was none other than Dr Septacemius J. Septic! The ruthless maniac whose acts of violence, cruelty and wickedness had struck terror into the hearts of animals and decent folk for decades. And into Johnny's own heart, ever since he was knee-high to a guinea pig.

28

As skinny as spaghetti and clad in a black leather trench coat, rhino-hide riding boots and leopard-skin jodhpurs, the mad and misguided maniac was sprawled across a blood-red, velvet settee, his mouth twisted into a sneer of hatred. Around his neck hung a doctor's stethoscope and, at his side, a false hand poked out from his coat sleeve.

With his other, real hand, Dr Septic was affectionately stroking the cat which lay curled in his lap. The cat which was identical to Wayne Bunn's beloved moggy Felix Pawson. That cat was none other than Felix's wayward and utterly ne'er-do-well twin brother Roland.

The Roland who Dr Septic had adopted as his own, having kitnapped the twin kittens and imprisoned them in the experimental laboratories of the wicked St Bernard Muttshoes (but that's another story✻).

✻ *See Johnny Catbiscuit to the Rescue!*

CHAPTER THREE
THE PARTY POOPER

As the hissing and jeering was replaced by a stunned silence, Dr Septic stopped stroking Roland and wagged a menacing finger at the flabber-smacked superheroes. 'Thought that might surprise you!' he rasped in a voice which made the superheroes think of an alligator gargling with broken glass. 'I'm sure I'm the last person you want turning up at your cosy little "get-together". Especially with you all feeling

so *pleeeeased* with yourselves. You sickeningly self-satisfied set of **SWAGGERiNG SMUGGERMUGS!**'

Johnny Catbiscuit and Felix Pawson exchanged appalled glances, horrified that their first ever **GOSH** Awards should end in such a shocking way.

'But your self-satisfaction doesn't surprise me!' continued Dr Septic, tickling Roland behind the ears. 'You've all had an exceptionally successful year. As I know, to my cost!'

'Well, in that case, consider yourself well and truly trounced!' yelled Captain Unstoppable, leaping to his feet and shaking his silicon-sheathed fist at the menacing mishmash of

light rays, radio waves and pixels which was the virtual Dr Septic. 'And leave us to enjoy ourselves. We haven't even had the party games yet. You loathsome reptile, you!'

'Hear, hear!' yelled the superheroes. 'Be off with you, you slimesome and wicked man!'

'**OH NO, NO, NO, NO, NO . . . NO!**' admonished Dr Septic, furiously wagging his finger at them. 'Having taken the trouble to cybernetically interfere in your "smugfest", I'm not about to go, just so you lot can play "What's the time, Mr Werewolf?" or whatever you silly billys get up to!'

'No, *I'm* Silly Billy!' shouted Silly Billy,

who was now seated amongst the guests. *'They're* all superheroes!'

'I do realise that, you insufferable little shop-keeper!' snarled Dr Septic. 'It may have escaped your notice, but **I AM A BLINKING GENIUS!** You simple-minded fashion fiasco! I've seen rubbish tips with better dress-sense than you!'

The smooth-as-silk Roland nodded, then hissed at Silly Billy. The joke-shop owner buried his face in his hands, instantly devastated by Dr Septic's razor-edged wit.

'I say, there's no call for that sort of talk!' muttered a few of the superheroes.

But Dr Septic paid them no heed. He was too

busy cranking up his inner infuriometer to rage-mark one hundred! 'And being a pointy-head of such terrifying intelligence,' he ranted, tapping his pale and bony skull, 'I know all sorts of STUFF! For instance, I know that for Space-Speck Earth to work the way the Great Mischief Maker in the Skyosphere intended, us baddies have to get a look in now and again!'

Roland stood up and arched his back, then spat contemptuously and deliberately in the direction of the superheroes. Then he curled up again, and went to sleep.

'**BOO BOOO BOOOO!**' the superheroes all roared. '**TRIPE, PIFFLE AND BALDERDASH!**'

'You lot have had it your own way for too long!' screamed Dr Septic. 'It's high time me and my lot set things to wrongs! Especially as that pair of sticky-beaks down there have spent the last year ruining every single one of my ingenious and wicked schemes!'

Realising Dr Septic was talking about himself and Felix, Johnny spoke up. 'But that's what we're supposed to do, Dr Septic!' he protested. 'We're superheroes! And anyway, have you never thought of turning your amazing talents to good use, such as developing an infinitely sustainable non-polluting bio-fuel, or finding a cure for Spraddlington's Hairy Tongue disease?

Rather than spending your days dreaming up more ways to make people miserable!'

'Hear, hear!' the superheroes cheered.

'Oh, go boil your brains, superboy!' snarled Dr Septic. 'I've had it up to here with you and that four-legged bottom-licker you call a sidekick! You . . . you . . . Johnny-come-lately!'

But then, as Roland briefly opened one eye and sneered at his twin brother, Dr Septic's rage suddenly stopped. With a scornful smirk replacing his savage scowl, he said, 'You lot just don't get it, do you? Listen! If I were a stick of seaside rock I'd have the word **EVIL** written all the way though me. Doing bad stuff is what I

was made for!' Then he said, 'Hmmm, I feel good now that I've got that off my chest. And, as the atmosphere is now somewhat, er . . . anti-Septic, I think it's high time we were off!'

'You've always been off, Dr Septic!' yelled Captain Unstoppable. 'Off your rocker!'

Unfazed by Captain Unstoppable's joke, and ignoring the laughter which echoed around the hall, Dr Septic leaned back on his virtual settee, hands clasped behind his head in an attitude of supreme self-confidence. Then he delivered his final words. 'OK, party-people! I will leave you with this thought.' He paused, sneered, then said, 'Knowledge is power!' after which he

winked, adding, 'Isn't it . . . Alan?'

As the images of Dr Septic and his cat faded from the **iPOdiUM**™, the superheroes stared at one another in bewilderment. Apart from two of them. One was a very old, retired superhero, who, not quite grasping the difference between

the virtual and the real Dr Septic, yelled, **'DON'T LET HIM GET AWAY!'** then hurled himself at the disappearing 3D likeness, only to pass right through it and fall in a heap. And the other was the Silver Ripple. He had turned as white as a snowflake. And was looking utterly horrified!

'So what do you think *that* was all about?' said Felix, as puzzled groups of superheroes gathered to discuss Dr Septic's staggering cyber-intrusion. 'And who's this "Alan"?'

'I haven't the faintest idea,' replied Johnny. 'But I've a feeling we're going to find out soon!'

He wasn't wrong.

CHAPTER FOUR

DR NOOT

The following Saturday morning, Wayne Bunn
was tucking into his bowl of Wakey Flakeys™
when his gran said, 'Oh dear, the poor chap! I
hope he's all right. Always so polite. And such
warm hands. What I call a real gentleman!'

Wayne was puzzled, but then she held up the
Nicetown Advertiser. Wayne read the article
on the front page.

NICETOWN
Advertiser

MYSTERIOUS DISAPPEARANCE:
LOCAL DOCTOR NOT SEEN FOR DAYS
PATIENTS 'SICK' WITH WORRY

Friends and family of Dr Alan Noot, MD. BSc, of Moon Lane, Clammy Bottom, are very concerned. Dr Noot (32), father of four, amateur table-tennis player and Chairman of the Clammy Bottom Jogging Club, hasn't been seen for several days.

'He left home on Wednesday to jog to work through Clammy Bottom Woods,' said his wife, Annabelle (31). 'But then I got a call from Nicetown Health Centre, saying he'd not turned up. At first, I didn't worry, as Alan frequently gets called away on urgent business, often for days at a time. But he

42

always calls me. It's so unlike him not to have been in touch. I do hope he's OK!'

Police Inspector Hector Vector said, 'I'm not too worried. I know Alan to be a very capable chap. Not to mention an ace ping-pong player! I thrashed him 6–4, only last week. But that may have been because of his hand injury. He got it whilst examining a small boy who'd swallowed his mum's car keys. The boy bit him.'

STOP PRESS: Inspector Vector has asked us to point out that it was the boy's mum's car keys which were swallowed. Not Dr Noot's mum's car keys.

STOP STOP PRESS: Dr Noot's medical bag has just been found in Clammy Bottom Woods. When asked about this, Inspector Vector said, 'I am looking into it.'

43

Three minutes later, Wayne and Felix were in his gran's garden shed, the newspaper spread out in front of them.

'It's him,' said Wayne, quickly slipping on his silver 'JC' vest and adjusting his biometric, plasma-chuffed wrist-pod. 'It's got to be!'

'What makes you so sure?' said Felix. 'There must be *thousands* of Alans in the Realms of Normality!'

'It's this bit where Inspector Vector mentions Dr Noot's injured hand,' said Wayne. 'Remember what the Silver Ripple said when he dropped his golden **WHOOSH!** award?'

'He said he'd had his fingers nibbled by a small boy!' exclaimed Felix. 'Sweaty spaghetti! I think you're on to something!'

'I *know* I'm on to something!' said Wayne. 'Dr Noot *is* the Silver Ripple!'

'But do you think we should even be discussing this?' said Felix, looking round nervously. 'We're not supposed to know the

45

other superheroes' day-to-day identities!'

'Exactly, FP!' exclaimed Wayne. 'It's absolutely crucial that we all live our non-super lives in total anonymity. With our everyday identities in the clutches of Dr Septic, we'd be space-dust before that murderous maniac could say, "I know where you live!"'

'And you think Dr Septic has discovered that Dr Noot is the Silver Ripple?'

'I'm certain of it! Especially when I think of how Dr Septic said, "Knowledge is power!" then looked at the Silver Ripple as he said, "Isn't it, Alan?",' replied Wayne. He pulled on his winged boots. 'I just hope we can get to the

Ripple before *he* becomes space-dust!'

He stood up, took a deep breath, put his hands on his hips and said:

> 'Dr Septic's up to tricks.
> The Ripple's in a fix.
> So we'll sort this little teaser,
> Then ZAP that evil geezer!'

And, once more, Wayne Bunn transformed from a scrawny twelve-year-old schoolboy into handsome superhero and vanquisher of all that is wicked: **JOHNNY CATBISCUIT!**

'OK, superboy!' purred Felix, as he transformed into a super sidekick. 'Let's go and talk to our old friend Inspector Vector!'

47

'We will!' said Johnny. 'We will! But first . . . Jatinder!' He flipped his wrist-pod into 'communicate' mode, then tapped in *W-0000-SH*, pressed the hash key and chose *OPTION 6*.

A microsecond later his cyber-kick's face appeared on the 3D screen. 'Hi, Johnny!' she said. 'Thank you for calling Superhero Support Service Solutions. And congratulations on the award! Now, how may I help you?'

'Hi, Jatinder!' said Johnny. 'I need some info on the people who have access to the secret dossiers on every superhero in the Realms.'

'Sure!' said Jatinder. 'The super-profilers. But I must warn you. We're getting reports

48

of an incident in downtown Chipchester. So we might be interrupted.'

'OK, we'll keep it brief!' said Johnny. 'We're somewhat busy ourselves.'

'Right!' said Jatinder. 'The dossiers are stored at the S.S.S.S.S.S.S.S.S.S.S.'

'I beg your pardon!' exclaimed Felix, his fur suddenly bristling.

'The Superhero Support Service Solutions Strategically Sited Super Sphere Secret

Statistic Storage Station!' said Jatinder.

'Ah, got you!' said Felix. 'For one moment, I thought you were hissing!'

'It's the place you know as Silly Billy's,' said Jatinder.

'The home of the Great Hall of Superhero Fame!' said Felix.

'And the HQ for the boys who keep our Super-Show on the road!' said Jatinder. 'In other words, those guys in white coats in Silly Billy's basement re-energising power-belts, mending invisibility cloaks, re-spangling super-suits and dreaming up new super-gadgets.'

'Whilst fiddling with smoke bombs and fake

dog poo, to make it look like they really are working in a joke shop!' said Johnny.

'Precisely!' said Jatinder. 'And working alongside them are the super-profilers, who have access to the top-secret superhero dossiers containing all-important data: their super-specialisms; their rescue histories; Super-Sphere status; transformation rhymes; shoe sizes, and much more.'

'Including,' said Johnny, 'the details of the superheroes' day-to-day identities? Like my own and Felix's. Or . . . the Silver Ripple's?'

'Definitely!' said Jatinder. 'And, just as importantly, lists of any personal weaknesses

which might leave you superheroes in danger!'

'So,' said Johnny, 'if that information fell into the wrong hands, that superhero would be maniac-meat before you could say . . . **KERPOW!**'

'Absolutely!' said Jatinder. 'But there's no chance of that. Once processed, the digitally encrypted secret data is embedded in the most innocent-looking novelties. Things like whoopee cushions and tubes of trick toothpaste. And, as an extra safeguard, it's all fragmented! It would take a genius to decipher and piece together all that superhero data!'

'Possibly . . . an evil genius?' said Johnny. 'For instance, Dr Septic? A dodgy super-profiler

52

could hand him the secret information.'

'No chance!' said Jatinder. 'I'd trust those super-profilers with my life.'

'Well, I'm afraid you might well be making a mistake then, Jatinder!' said Johnny. 'Because it's looking very much like someone has betrayed us. I'm 99.999 per cent certain that Dr Septic is now in possession of information from at least one of those secret dossiers!'

'You're kidding!' exclaimed Jatinder. 'Whose secret file?'

'The one belonging to the –'

But before Johnny could finish, Jatinder interrupted him, saying, 'Hang on! I've got an

urgent call coming in.'

Johnny suddenly got the feeling that this was bad news, connected with what they'd just been talking about. He wasn't wrong!

Jatinder's face turned ashen and her eyes widened with horror. 'It's Captain Unstoppable!' she gasped. 'Something terrible's happened!'

CHAPTER FIVE
BORIS AND BETTY

'Now, Jatinder, let me get this straight!' said Johnny. He was shocked by the terrible news Jatinder had just given him but was determined to remain calm (like the true superhero he was). 'All heck broke loose in downtown Chipchester. And Captain Unstoppable went to sort it out. But now that fearless and unflappable superhero is crouched in a shop doorway,

quivering like a jelly, and saying that he wants his mummy?'

'It's worse than that!' blurted out Jatinder. 'He's sobbing like a five-year-old!'

'Bouncing bathmats!' muttered Felix. 'What can be going on?'

An image of Dr Septic saying, 'Knowledge is power!' flashed into Johnny's mind, but his thoughts were interrupted by more bad news from Jatinder.

'And there's something else,' she continued. 'I've just been told that one of our most experienced superheroes – THE SILVER RIPPLE – is missing! Johnny, we need your help. Fast!'

And so Felix **LEAPT** into Johnny's backpack and then, with the grace of a sparrowhawk, plus a flick of his super-heels, Johnny launched the pair of them skywards. An instant later, the dynamic duo were **ROCKETING** over the fields and villages of the Realms of Normality, super-speeding towards Chipchester.

Three minutes later, Johnny and Felix arrived at the normally smart 'Mugs and Spenders' shopping hamlet in downtown Chipchester and witnessed scenes of disorder not seen since the Abominable Snotmen's terrifying invasion of Londonland. Street signs were mangled, water gushed from broken

fire-hydrants, children wept, grown-ups screamed, cats meowed, mice prayed, and dogs howled, all to a background of screeching burglar alarms and wailing police sirens.

It didn't take them long to spot the cause of all this chaos. It was the dreaded Bullwinkle twins: Bouncing Boris Bullwinkle, the Ten-Ton-Baby, and his twin sister, Big Betty Bullwinkle. The pair of them looked like **overgrown hippopotamuses** who'd accidentally wandered into a babywear shop.

Boris, his flabby folds of flesh wobbling like a vast, pink jelly, was wearing a fluffy white nappy the size of a tent, while Betty was togged

out in a knitted pink bonnet and romper suit, big enough to hide a flock of sheep in.

The twins were yet another of the outlandish creations Dr Septic used in his campaign of terror against the Realms of Normality. And they were having the time of their lives!

Boris was perched on top of a police car and enthusiastically bouncing up and down on its roof. Crouched inside it were four extremely unhappy-looking police officers, one of whom was no less an AIP* than Inspector Hector Vector, of the Metropolopitan Sector.

Meanwhile, Big Betty was interested in some unfortunate soul she'd trapped in a shop door-

* AIP: Averagely Important Person

way. An unfortunate soul who the pals now saw
was Captain Unstoppable!

As Johnny and Felix watched in horror,
Betty seized the blubbering superhero in her
massive pudgy fingers, stuffed his head into her
gigantic toothless mouth, and gave it a really
good suck! As quickly as Betty popped him in,

she pulled him out, with a sudden **PLOP!** So no serious damage was done.

But Captain Unstoppable, already a gibbering wreck, looked absolutely terrible, his head and shoulders dripping with fresh baby drool and his super-suit smeared with baby goo! And Betty wasn't finished. Obviously finding Captain Unstoppable to her taste, she grabbed him again, this time licking him furiously. Boris continued bouncing on the police car, which was now two-thirds flat!

'**LET'S DO IT, PARTNER!**' said Johnny. '**BREAK-DANCING CAT ROUTINE?**'

'**PURRFECT!**' purred Felix.

61

So, Felix helicoptered, head-spun, backflipped and broncoed in front of Betty. She cooed with delight and dropped Captain Unstoppable. Johnny grasped the seat of the giant infant's baby-gro, hiked her into the air, then whizzed her over to Chipchester Zoo, where he dropped her into the conveniently empty bear pit.

Boris didn't come nearly so quietly. Rather than being entertained by Felix's dancing, he simply grabbed him and attempted to swallow him whole! It was only Johnny's quick thinking which saved Felix.

Seizing a handy traffic cone, Johnny rushed at Boris yelling, 'Oochie coochie coo, look what I've got for you!', causing Boris to abandon Felix and open his big mouth just long enough for Johnny to ram the cone in it. This left Boris sitting there wide-eyed with surprise, sucking furiously on his new bright orange 'dummy'.

As the citizens of Chipchester cheered wildly, Johnny hoisted Boris into the air and flew him

off to a building site where he snagged his nappy elastic on the hook of a giant crane and left him dangling thirty metres high.

'Thanks, guys! You saved my bacon!' said Captain Unstoppable a few minutes later, having recovered three-quarters of his legendary cool. He'd also managed to wipe off most of Betty's slobber. 'Bit of a problem back there!'

'Can't say I noticed,' said Johnny, doing his

best to spare Captain Unstoppable his blushes.

'Me neither!' shrugged Felix.

'I'd normally have that pair sorted in a jiffy,'
went on Captain Unstoppable.

'Of course!' said Johnny.

'No-brainer!' agreed Felix.

'Caught me completely off my guard!' said
Captain Unstoppable, turning crimson and
staring shamefacedly at his super-boots. 'Not
had a turn like that since I was ooh, knee-high
to a ray-gun!'

'Er, what sort of turn?' said Johnny, suddenly
becoming very curious.

Captain Unstoppable went even redder then,

glancing around furtively, he put his hand over his mouth and whispered, 'Can I let you guys in on a secret? And, if I do, will you promise never to breathe a word of it to anyone? Superhero's honour?'

'Superhero's honour!' said Felix. 'Cross my paws and hope to fry!'

'Me too!' said Johnny.

'OK!' said Captain Unstoppable. Then he took a deep breath and said, 'I've got purplebrasproutophobia!'

'You've got purplebra . . . what?' exclaimed Felix.

'Purplebrasproutophobia!' mumbled Captain Unstoppable. 'That's its scientific name. It means I'm terrified of purple sprouting broccoli! Well, not all of it. Just the really rare sort which grows in the Panamazone Jungle!'

At this point, had Johnny and Felix been insensitive types, they would have been rolling around on the floor, hysterical with laughter. But they weren't, so they stifled their grins and tried to look as concerned as possible.

'Just one glimpse of the stuff turns me into a gibbering wreck,' continued Captain Unstoppable.

'It's all because of a very nasty incident when I was little. It took place in the dining-hall at Superhero Prep School and involved an entire panful of the stuff and an extremely stroppy dinner lady.' He shuddered, then said, 'But I don't really want to talk about that.'

'I'm sure you don't,' said Felix, giving Captain Unstoppable a pat on the shoulder.

'No one else in the entire world knows about it,' sniffed Captain Unstoppable. 'Apart from the super-profilers, of course.'

'Of course!' said Johnny.

'I mean,' went on Captain Unstoppable, 'what a coincidence! Boris and Betty turning

68

up like that, both clutching sprigs of purple sprouting broccoli. And not the ordinary type, but the very sort I'm so terrified of!'

'Yes,' said Felix. 'What a coincidence!'

But Johnny knew otherwise. Once more, an image of Dr Septic saying, 'Knowledge is power!' flashed through his mind. However, just as his lightning-fast brain was coming to some extremely disturbing conclusions, his thoughts were again interrupted by a very anxious Jatinder appearing on his wrist-pod, this time saying, 'Johnny, we've got another one! Over in Michaelsfield! It's Bodacious Babe. She's completely lost it!'

CHAPTER SIX
a TICKLISH SITUATION

Johnny and Felix heard Bodacious Babe's screams before they even got to Michaelsfield.

'Jatinder wasn't exaggerating!' said Felix, as the pals exchanged grim looks.

Two minutes later they were confronted by a shocking sight.

Perched on the roof of the Saint Rolfus of Ozissi Poorly Pet Sanctuary was Dr Septic's horrible hench-boy Spitting Cuthbert. In one

70

hand, he clutched a basket of howling puppies, about to hurl the sweet little things to their doom! In the other, he held a huge feathered tickling-stick with which he was mercilessly tormenting Bodacious Babe, causing her to shriek and howl and roll around, making her

helpless . . . with laughter!

'**GIBBERING JACKRABBITS!**' exclaimed Johnny.

'**CARTWHEELING CATERPILLARS!**' gasped Felix.

The two pals wasted no time.

WHOOSH! went Johnny, flashing towards Cuthbert at the speed of light. **ZAP!** went his right hand, as it knocked the tickling-stick flying. **THUNK!** went his left fist as he walloped Cuthbert squarely on the chin. **SNAP!** went Felix, as he snatched the plummeting basket of puppies out of mid-air.

The cowardly Cuthbert was outmatched and outclassed. Clutching his jaw, he fled the scene. He yelled, 'You ain't seen nothing yet,

Catbiscuit! Three cheers for Gluey Hughie!'

Had Johnny had a chance to give this parting shot greater attention, it might have given him cause for thought. But he was more concerned about the normally hard-as-nails and supremely sassy Bodacious Babe, who was no longer shrieking with laughter, but holding her head in her hands and sobbing uncontrollably!

'I'm a failure!' she groaned, as they watched the fleeing Cuthbert bound from rooftop to rooftop. 'He's made a complete fool of me! I'm not worthy of this purple-spangled superhero body stocking and silver spandex super-boots!'

'Now, now!' said Johnny, putting a comforting

74

arm around Bodacious Babe's broad and sparkly shoulders. 'None of us can be super the whole time. We all have our off days!'

'But this is more than an off day!' sniffed Bodacious Babe. Then, taking out her spangled handkerchief, she dabbed her tear-stained cheeks and said, 'It seems like someone's discovered my little weakness!'

'Let me guess!' said Felix. 'You're ticklish?'

'Yes, I am!' sobbed Bodacious Babe. 'But how did you know?'

'Just a hunch!' said Felix, with a shrug.

'And here's me thinking all that was behind me!' whimpered Bodacious Babe.

'All behind you, Bodacious Babe?' said Johnny. 'How so?'

'Well, Johnny!' sniffed Bodacious Babe. 'When I was first chosen to become "Super", the only thing holding me back from graduating with a first-class degree in Superiority and All-round Brilliance was my extreme ticklishness.'

'So they decided that you weren't "up-to-scratch"!' said Felix.

'Felix!' said Johnny. 'This is no time for jokes.'

'Sorry,' said Felix. 'Please carry on, Bodacious Babe.'

'My super-trainer put me on a de-tickliffication course,' went on Bodacious Babe. 'I was sub-

jected to every sort of tickling known to super-kind. Stroked with a tickling-whisk made from the chin-fluff of young choirboys! Pushed through a tunnel filled with wagging doggy tails. Caressed with a giant duster made from the transparent feathers of the Almost-Not-There Bird! They even made me wear a fluffy angora sweater inside-out for a month!'

'Nightmare!' said Felix.

'But, through sheer willpower,' went on Bodacious Babe, 'I finally made myself immune to every sort of ticklish material on Space-Speck Earth! Well, all except for the eyelashes of the Kandaharan Camelot!'

'The most ticklish thing known to person-kind,' said Johnny, picking up Cuthbert's tickling-stick and examining it thoughtfully.

'Exactly!' said Bodacious Babe. '"But hey!" I thought. "Who's gonna know about that?"'

'Well,' said Johnny, stroking the tickling-stick's Kandaharan Camelot eyelashes, 'it certainly looks like Spitting Cuthbert did.'

'But *how*?' said Bodacious Babe. 'Until today, apart from my Superhero School trainer, the only people who knew about my little secret were the super-profilers at Silly Billy's!'

Now Johnny was one hundred per cent certain! It wasn't just the Silver Ripple's secret

data which had fallen into Dr Septic's hands.
Captain Unstoppable's and Bodacious Babe's
had, too! He had to let Jatinder know that
there was a treacherous super-profiler who
had handed over the superheroes' secrets. And
perhaps even his own and Felix's!

If that was the case, every super-defender of
the Realms of Normality would now be at the
mercy of Dr Septic. They would be powerless
to carry out their superhero duties, leaving the
place they loved so much wide open to an
all-out attack from the evil genius and his
horrendous hordes. The animals, children and
grown-ups who inhabited that lovely land

79

would be in terrible, *terrible* danger!

But there was still a chance for him and Felix to save the day!

For Johnny knew that even someone as utterly brilliant as Dr Septic would still need time to decipher and piece together that great mass of coded data. Which gave him and Felix a very brief window of opportunity, not only to retrieve the stolen secrets, but also to save their good friend, the Silver Ripple. However, just as all this was sinking in, and Johnny was breathing a very cautious sigh of relief, he felt a hand on his shoulder, and heard a voice say, 'Ah, Mr Catbiscuit. I've finally got you!'

CHAPTER SEVEN
GLUEY HUGHIE!

It was Inspector Hector Vector, of the Metropolopitan Detector Sector. Bent completely double, he and his officers had driven their extremely squashed police car to Michaelsfield. Albeit very slowly!

Using his super-strength, it took Johnny just a few minutes to unsquash the car and smooth out its bumps and wrinkles. Inspector Vector was very grateful. He was also desperate to

thank Johnny and Felix for sorting out the Bullwinkle twins and Spitting Cuthbert.

But first, Johnny had to make his crucial call to Jatinder, telling her to alert all the other superheroes to the terrible danger they were in! And to urge her and her colleagues to do their utmost to root out the traitorous boffin who was passing secrets to Dr Septic!

Then, after making that vital call, he and Felix joined Inspector Vector in the Complete Mug Café, determined to come up with a plan to find Dr Noot. Or the Silver Ripple, as they preferred to think of him!

'Well done, Mr Catbiscuit!' gushed Inspector

Vector. 'I think we've seen the backs of Dr Septic's horrible hordes for some time!'

'I wouldn't bank on it!' said Johnny. 'That was just a test run. Dr Septic's horrors will soon return! And then, it will be the real deal!'

'Oh dear!' said Inspector Vector, suddenly

looking extremely anxious.

'How are your neck and shoulders?' said Felix, trying to distract him from his worries.

'Not too bad,' said Inspector Vector. 'But I'm very worried about my lob!'

'Very worried about your *what*?' said Felix.

'It's a table-tennis stroke,' said Johnny. 'He's worried about his game!'

'That's right!' said Inspector Vector. Then he sighed, saying, 'I shouldn't moan! At least I'll play again. Which is more than I can say for poor Dr Noot!'

'The very person we want to talk about!' said Johnny. 'How's your investigation going?'

'Well,' said Inspector Vector, 'we've had the sniffer dogs in Clammy Bottom Woods again.'

'Any leads?' said Felix.

'Oh no, we don't have them on leads!' said Inspector Vector. 'We just let them rush around all over the place. That way, there's more chance of them finding something!'

'I think he means, did they discover any clues?' said Johnny.

'Oh, I see!' said Inspector Vector. 'Well, so far, just Dr Noot's medical bag. I was hoping it might contain some crucial evidence. But I'd hardly begun looking into it when I got stuck!'

'You came up against a brick wall?' said

Johnny Catbiscuit.

'Oh, no!' said Inspector Vector. 'I got stuck as in, glued solid! That pesky bag was covered in super-sticky gunge. Once I'd picked it up, I couldn't put it down. It took my chaps ages to get me free. And even now, I've still got this!'

He held out his hand. To the pals' astonishment, attached to it was the strap of Dr Noot's

medical bag!

'Oh dear,' joked Felix. 'Now you haven't even got a handle on the case!'

And, despite the gravity of the situation, he and Inspector Vector laughed.

But Johnny Catbiscuit wasn't laughing. Something had suddenly begun furiously nudging at one of the billions of supercharged memory-nodes in his awesomely powerful hyper-brain. But, try as he might, he couldn't quite unlock the thought-capsule holding the piece of data which was now screaming, 'Johnny Catbiscuit, look at me!'

Then, getting into the pun'n'games, Inspector Vector said, 'Yes, this whole investigation is turning out to be a sticky wicket!'

To which Felix replied, 'I'm afraid you're just

going to have to *stick* with it!'

Which was when a light-bulb the size of a warning beacon lit up inside Johnny's brain. Flipping open his wrist-pod, he tapped in his **SSSS** user code. 'Jatinder!' he said, as his cyber-kick appeared. 'I owe you an apology. I don't think there is a traitor in Silly Billy's basement, after all! But, just to be one hundred per cent certain, I need to know something. Silly Billy said someone had played a prank on him. And left him in a fix! What sort of a fix?'

'Some joker put super-gloo on his chair,' said Jatinder.

Johnny's super-brain immediately did the

following computation:

Then he yelled, 'Gluey Hughie!'

'I beg your pardon!' said the waitress, who was just putting down their biscuits.

'Gluey Hughie!' repeated Felix, leaping aboard Johnny's speeding train of thought.

'Gluey Hughie!' said Inspector Vector, doing his best to sound like he knew what was going on.

'Gluey Hughie!' said Jatinder, who remained connected via Johnny's wrist-pod.

'Oh, yes – Gluey Hughie!' said the waitress, who still hadn't the foggiest what any of them were talking about.

'Yes – Gluey Hughie!' said the Silver Ripple, as he walked into the Complete Mug Café with Gluey Hughie slung over his shoulder. 'I think this is the chap everyone's talking about!'

CHAPTER EIGHT
THE CONFESSION

'How did you do it, Silver Ripple?' said Johnny, as Inspector Vector rushed off to brief his men, leaving Johnny and Felix (and for that matter, Gluey Hughie), regarding the Silver Ripple with undisguised awe and admiration.

'I'm not Superhero of the Year for nothing!' said the Silver Ripple, stirring his tea and nodding at Gluey Hughie. 'All right, so this young chap did take me by surprise as I jogged

92

through Clammy Bottom Woods.'

Gluey Hughie smirked.

'And he got me stuck with a huge blast of super-gloo. And he also knew that in order to transform, I must be holding something silver. So he dumped my medical bag with its silver instruments. And took away my penknife and everything else silver! But then he made his stupid mistake, didn't you, Hughie?'

Gluey Hughie nodded glumly.

'As he was driving his little van back to Dr Septic's place, he just couldn't resist stopping off and buying some chocolate with the change he'd taken from my pocket. And, being a litter

lout, he dropped the silver wrapper. Which is when I turned the tables on him!'

'Brilliant!' said Johnny and Felix in unison.

'But what still puzzles me, is how on Space-Speck Earth he discovered my secret identity?' the Silver Ripple said.

'We know,' said Johnny.

'Gluey Hughie's been stealing secrets!' declared Felix.

'The sneaky rascal!' exclaimed the Silver Ripple.

'But what we need to know,' said Johnny, 'is how?'

'And for that matter, why?' said Felix.

'Yes, why did you do it, Gluey Hughie?' said Johnny.

'To prove to Dad that I'm not completely useless!' said Gluey Hughie. 'I'm sure he loves that cat Roland more than he loves me!'

'Which isn't surprising,' said Felix. 'After all, he is extremely good-looking!'

'Well, as you know,' continued Gluey Hughie, 'I'm a real sucker for disguises and pranks and I'm forever hanging around joke shops, including Silly Billy's! Which is how I realised things weren't all they seemed. So I investigated. Which was a doddle. All I had to do was kidnap the chap from **CLEAN IT!**™.'

95

'The Information Technology Hygiene Services,' said Johnny.

'Yep! I pinched his van, uniform and ID chip. And I was in!'

'But how did you know the secrets were stashed in the tricks?' said Johnny.

'I didn't! I just pinched them. Dad had stopped my pocket money after my mass super-glooing disaster and I was desperate for some new pranks. It was only after I put my new whoopee cushion on his favourite chair and he went ballistic and ripped it to pieces that we discovered the embedded microchip!'

'I bet he was chuffed!' said Felix.

'Not half!' said Gluey Hughie. 'I was suddenly his favourite person ever! He even banished Roland to his kennel for "meowing inappropriately". I can tell you, he is not a happy cat!' Then Gluey Hughie frowned. 'But it won't last. Dad still loves Roland more than me!'

'You poor thing!' said Felix.

'Anyway,' said Gluey Hughie, 'when he cracked the first cipher and discovered

the Silver Ripple's day-to-day identity, Dad was ecstatic!'

'Which is when he sent you back to Silly Billy's to alter the settings on the **iPOdiUM**™ so that he could appear in place of Hillman Avenger!' said Johnny.

'And give us superheroes his "Knowledge is power!" message!' added the Ripple with a wry grin.

'But then you made your stupid mistake!' said Felix.

'Yes,' said Gluey Hughie. 'I just couldn't resist a prank before I left. So I squirted a blob of super-gloo on Silly Billy's chair.'

'Which alerted me to the fact it was you who'd stolen the secrets, and not a super-profiler!' said Johnny. 'If not for that we could have wasted days trying to discover the traitor at Silly Billy's!'

'And in the meantime, Dr Septic would have had time to crack all the ciphers and had all us superheroes at his mercy!' said Felix.

'I thought you were a sidekick?' said Gluey Hughie.

'I am,' said Felix, looking somewhat put out. 'But the point is, we still have a chance to save the Realms from your horrible stepdad!'

'And did Dr Septic send you to capture me?'

asked the Ripple.

'No, that was my idea!' Gluey Hughie said proudly. 'He doesn't even know yet. I thought I'd make a surprise present of you!'

'Well, he's not going to be pleased when he discovers you've failed yet again,' said Johnny. 'I think you're about to become his least favourite person again, Hughie! How far along is he with the deciphering?'

'When I last saw him he was decoding the info on Captain Unstoppable and Bodacious Babe. He says once he cracks the master cipher, the rest will be a piece of cake!'

'We need to pay him an urgent visit!' said

Johnny. 'I've got an idea!'

But before Johnny told his pals about his idea, he turned to Hughie and said, 'Hughie, I'm going to toss a coin! If it comes up tails we let you go. But if it comes up heads, you help us with our plan! Then we let you go!'

'All right!' said Hughie, still upset his stepdad preferred Roland. 'Sounds fair enough to me!'

So Johnny tossed the coin and it came up heads. Hughie shrugged and said, 'OK, what do you want me to do?' And Johnny told him.

Hardly had Johnny finished outlining his plans and explaining to Hughie just what would happen to him if he didn't co-operate, when

Inspector Vector returned.

'Gentlemen!' he said importantly. 'I've put my men on the highest state of alert. And I've also issued a statement to the press saying that

the security situation in the Realms has been put up to "threat-level-orange-with-a-subtle-hint-of-avocado", due to information received from an undisclosed source!' Then he winked at Johnny and said, 'That's you, Mr Catbiscuit!'

'I'd sort of guessed that!' said Johnny.

But Inspector Vector wasn't listening. He was busy giving the Silver Ripple his long-and-hard policeman's stare and saying, 'I hope you don't mind me asking, Mr Ripple, but do you ever play table tennis?'

'No, never!' said the Ripple. 'Can't stand the stupid game.'

CHAPTER NINE
NEIGH!

Twenty minutes later, Gluey Hughie drove the little **CLEAN IT!**™ van on to the driveway of an unassuming, but absolutely huge bungalow in rural Nothinghamshire. This unassuming but absolutely huge bungalow concealed the vast and complex network of kitchens, bathrooms, lounges, bedrooms, laboratories, corridors, computer suites, workshops, prison cells and 'interrogation' chambers which

housed Dr Septic and his army of vicious thugs. In other words, his current and temporary HQ in the Realms of Normality.

As Hughie was bundling the Silver Ripple out of the van and marching him up to the front door, his extremely wicked stepfather was feeling very, very excited! He was about to begin deciphering yet another chip-load of scintillating superhero secrets. And this particular nugget of stolen knowledge was exciting him more than any other. Because he'd now deduced that the lump of fake dog poo which lay in front him contained the secrets of his most hated (and feared) arch-enemy, Johnny

Catbiscuit! So, not only was he about to discover Johnny's true identity, but he was also about to find out all the little weaknesses which would render Johnny powerless in his hands!

There was a knock on the door and some of his burly hyper-thugs ushered in his dimwitted stepson Gluey Hughie. Dr Septic was not pleased. But then, when his *utterly brilliant and go-getting* stepson was followed into the room by the super-glooed and tightly-trussed award-winning superhero the Silver Ripple, he nearly punched the air and yelled, 'Way to go, Gluey Hughie. What a prize, my boy!'

But he didn't. Because he was, after all, Dr

Septacemius J. Septic, the most evil and cold-hearted villain on Space-Speck Earth. And he did have his image to think about. So what he *did* do was to ask Hughie what had kept him, then order his hyper-thugs to take the Silver Ripple along to the 'interrogation' chamber.

But now he was faced with a dilemma! Should he begin interrogating the Ripple because he might be in possession of information which would save him tons of time and trouble in his decrypting task? Or should he begin extracting the information about Johnny Catflap from the dollop of fake dog's doings?

The pull of the freshly-caught prey was too much! With a swift, muttered, 'Oh, super-heroes!', Dr Septic rushed along to the room where his thugs were 'softening up' the Silver Ripple in preparation for his 'interrogation'.

Hardly had Dr Septic hurried down that long corridor when, unheard by him, the doorbell

rang. It was answered by more of his horrible hyper-thugs. But when they looked out, there was no one there. Just as they were about to close the door, they heard a 'meow!' and looked down to see Roland sitting at their feet, looking all appealing and strokeable.

'Roland! You naughty pussy!' said a thug. 'You're supposed to be shut up in your kennel!'

And he reached down to pick up 'Roland'. But 'Roland' was in the mood for fun! So a second later he was scampering around the front garden with the four goons in hot pursuit.

Which gave Johnny Catbiscuit the chance to slip through the open front door, then make

his way along the corridor until his super-instincts told him he'd reached the room which contained the stolen secrets.

Meanwhile, in the 'interrogation' room, Dr Septic wasn't getting very far with the Silver Ripple, who was remarkably resilient to the Chinese burns, nose tweaks and dead-legs which the thugs were giving him.

'**OH, DRAGON'S BREATH!**' exclaimed the frustrated Dr Septic. 'Leave him be, he'll keep till later! I've got more important things to do!'

And he rushed back to his 'nugget of knowledge'. Absolutely desperate to unmask and defeat his hated foe, he seized the fake dog

poo containing those vital secrets, intent on tearing it apart. And he got a very unpleasant surprise. Because, rather than gripping the springy plastic of the trick dog's doings, his

fingers (both false and real) sank into something extremely squidgy and smelly! Yes! While Dr Septic had been out of the room, the fake dog poo had somehow turned into REAL dog poo! And he was now up to his knuckles in the stuff!

But it doesn't take a man of Dr Septic's genius long to realise there's trouble afoot! So, pausing only to thoroughly wash his hands, he punched the 'intruder-lock-in' alarm button and rushed from the room. Which is when Johnny Catbiscuit slipped out of his hiding place and finished making his substitutions. Then he went to work on the computer in which Dr Septic had stored all the superhero

secrets he'd discovered so far.

The plan was that Johnny would make all the changes, then join the Silver Ripple and Felix (or 'Roland', if you're a thug) out in the garden, and escape. This would leave Gluey Hughie free to gloo again, just as they'd promised. But only if he kept his part of the bargain – to pretend he'd bagged the Ripple.

And everything would have gone brilliantly. If it hadn't been for Gluey Hughie! Because, just as the alarms were screeching and thugs were pouring into the corridors from all directions, he had a change of heart. Seizing Dr Septic by the lapels of his long black snakeskin

smock, he yelled, 'Pater! It's all my fault. I've betrayed you. And I can't do that! Even if you are loathsome, evil and ruthless, I love you! After all, you are still fifty per cent my daddy, *Daddy*! Johnny Catbiscuit's here, in the bungalow! And the Ripple's not even properly glooed. He's only slightly sticky!'

Just then the Silver Ripple raced into the corridor, chased by the thugs to whom he'd just given a thorough slapping (in exchange for the Chinese burns), and Johnny Catbiscuit hurtled out of the computer room, having successfully accomplished his tasks.

It was now that Gluey Hughie had his

moment of glory. Thrusting aside his stepdad with a cry of, 'Leave this one to me, half-father!', he whipped out an enormous tube of super-gloo and let fly at Johnny and the Ripple. In seconds the two of them were coated in thick industrial-strength adhesive! Something they would have made short work of (just as the Silver Ripple had done earlier that day), had not a horde of hyper-thugs all piled on top of them, pinning them to the floor!

Gluey Hughie stood back, hands on hips, proudly surveying his handiwork. Handiwork, which in weeks to come, could well get him back in his half-dad's good books.

But right now, Dr Septic was disliking Gluey Hughie almost as much as he disliked super-heroes. So, he banished him to his bedroom and vowed not only to stop his pocket money forever, but also to make him pay back all the pocket money he'd ever had. Then he commanded his thugs to carry Johnny and the Ripple to the 'interrogation' room and begin 'preparing them'!

Next Dr Septic took a few moments to reflect upon the events of the last fifteen minutes, gazing wistfully out of the window. He felt betrayed and very much regretted having had the ever-loyal Roland locked up in his kennel.

At this point a familiar and much-loved face pressed itself up against the window and a little paw tapped on the glass. It was his beloved Roland! Dr Septic rushed to the front door to let him in. And he came face to face, not with Roland, but with Captain Unstoppable and Bodacious Babe! Dr Septic realised he'd just been duped for the third time that day. He instantly assumed the lethal '**FONG KWOK**' defensive stance.

But right now, Captain Unstoppable and Bodacious Babe weren't too bothered about Dr Septic. They were more intent on saving Johnny and the Ripple. So they charged off

down the corridor, super-fists windmilling in readiness to deal out superhero justice.

There now followed a most almighty scrap between hyper-thugs and superheroes. When it was finally depicted in comic strip form on the walls of the Great Superhero Hall of Fame, the writers and artists had to send out for lorry-loads of extra **ZAPs**, **KERPOWs** and **SPLATTs**, and emergency supplies of exclamation marks and bright red ink, such was its fury!

And, as that battle raged, the ever-realistic Dr Septic decided that it was time to be making himself scarce. So, having collected his stepson from his bedroom, he and Gluey Hughie

gathered up the computer and the stolen secrets and made ready to hightail it in the little white van. But then Dr Septic remembered his beloved Roland and rushed off in search of him, while Hughie kept the engine running.

When he eventually found Roland having a furious argument with himself outside his now-open kennel, the 'cat'-fluent Dr Septic

immediately thought of the cloning experiments he'd carried out in past years and began to wonder just how many 'Rolands' he actually possessed.

'Oh don't give me all that "what would Mum think" malarkey!' said one of the Rolands, bristling irritably. 'You always were a do-gooding little creep! What with your "let's be kinder to birds", "not bite the heads off baby mice", and "treat our owner's furniture with respect" ideas. When I think of the times you grassed me up to Mum, it makes me want to spit!'

And then this very stroppy Roland did spit! Right in the face of the other Roland. But the other Roland was completely unfazed, saying,

'But, bro'! It's never too late! Blood's thicker than water! We go back a long way. Why don't you start this life afresh and make up for your past cat-alogue of wrongdoing? Dump that sleazeball lowlife and come with me!'

Dr Septic let out a low growl, realising that he was the 'sleazeball' being referred to, and the 'do-gooding' Roland spotted him and instantly shot behind a bush. At which point Dr Septic remembered that Roland had once had a twin brother. So when the other Roland re-emerged as Johnny Catbiscuit's sidekick Felix Pawson, all suddenly became clear to him.

Snatching up the real Roland, Dr Septic

thrust him out in front of himself, using his lap-cat as a feline-shield, sure in the knowledge that Felix wouldn't harm his own brother. Which, of course, was entirely correct! But then, as Felix dodged and dived, doing his utmost to detain Dr Septic, while avoiding harming Roland, there was a screech of tyres and the little white van raced towards them with its passenger door wide open and Gluey Hughie yelling, 'Jump in, beloved stepDaddy!'

And with surprising agility for a villain of his age, Dr Septic did just that, and they were off in a cloud of exhaust fumes and cat fur, leaving Felix Pawson clutching at thin air while listening

to Roland yell, 'See you later, villain hater! We gotta go! Cheerio, my goody-goody bro'!'

So Dr Septic got away. And, arriving at Septic Towers, he once more began deciphering the stolen superhero secrets. And this time he was not only delighted to discover that they emerged with surprising ease, but also that the superhero-secrets' computer files contained some data which he'd not noticed when he'd first added it. But he put that down to the excitement of the moment and the tremendous pressure he'd been working under. Now armed with a rich batch of secret data, he set about making the superheroes' lives a misery!

But it only took a couple of very embarrassing incidents to make him realise he'd been duped

yet again! The first was when Danger Dude was confronted by Spitting Cuthbert waving a pair of fluffy slippers at him and yelling, '**FISH-PASTE! FISH-PASTE!**' at the top of his voice. The Dude assumed Cuthbert had taken leave of his senses, shrugged his shoulders and gave him the (fish) pasting he deserved. ***BASH!***

And the second was when Gluey Hughie kidnapped an ancient horse, believing it to be the real identity of the *FLYING FURY*, then transporting it back to Septic Towers. Dr Septic interrogated it mercilessly with questions like, 'Are you a superhero?' and, 'Is there really a Secret Superhero Training School?' To which

the horse shook its head and said 'Neigh!' every single time. Dr Septic was eventually convinced that all of the 'secrets' were complete piffle. Johnny Catfish had swapped them.

So he abandoned his stolen secrets project and began working on a new scheme to overthrow the Realms. This one was so cunning, so evil, and so completely foolproof that he just knew it would work. He rubbed his hands with glee at the prospect of destroying Johnny Catbiscuit and his furry sidekick very, *very* slowly.

As Felix and Johnny watched Dr Septic's stolen

secrets scheme come to naught, Felix got round to asking Johnny the question which had been puzzling him for some time.

'Why did you risk Gluey Hughie agreeing to your plan on the throw of a coin, Johnny?' he said.

Johnny replied, 'Wise up, partner! As if I would! Silly Billy's doesn't just stock whoopee cushions and chattering teeth, you know!'

Then, reaching into his pocket, he took out a double-headed coin and said, 'I'm even prepared to bet on it!'

THE END

Gluey Hughie

Practical joker, chocolate addict and master of disguises, Hugh Desmond Evil Junior (19), or 'Gluey Hughie', as he's more commonly know, is the only son of Janice Evil and the 'stepson' of her partner, Dr Septic.

PHYSICAL APPEARANCE

He's five foot three inches tall, with an enormous shock of bright blue hair, very prominent front teeth and, undisguised, is fond of wearing the sort of clothes that make it

hard to miss him in a crowd, e.g. bright purple suits with day-glo yellow shirts, sequinned scarlet ties and pink, alligator-skin, winkle-picker shoes. When he isn't tootling around in stolen white vans, he cruises the highways in a massively 'be-finned' lime-green Kaddilslik Supakrooza™, playing deafening Rhythm 'n' Roll music.

CHILDHOOD

Ever since his mum can recall, Hughie has been a mischievous and energetic individual and is now living up to all her hopes and dreams, i.e. being the utter slacker and double-crossing ne'er-do-well she's proud

130

to call 'son'. However, Hughie did go through a very 'difficult' patch. For several months, he showed signs of 'wanting to be good'. During this worrying time, Hughie was kind and considerate to others, always taking into account their feelings and making their well-being his priority. Janice was at her wits' end. But, with dogged determination, and a lot of help from Dr Septic, Janice eventually overcame Hughie's difficulty, telling him off if he patted a dog or offered one of his chocolates to another child. And finally, after an intense course of hypnotherapy, and 'fiendishness implants' from Dr Septic, Hughie was soon

causing havoc and unhappiness, and rewarded for his trouble-making with lots of chocolate.

EVIL DEEDS

Gluey Hughie is obsessed with practical jokes, especially those involving super-gloo and all things sticky: solder, sealing wax, bird lime, gum arabic, chewing gum, paste and water, even garlic juice! Hughie's tried them all! His earliest adhesiventure involved smearing super-gloo all over the running track on his school sports day (apart from his own lane, of course) which resulted in all the other boys appearing to run in slow motion, while Hughie belted round and won. After that

there was no stopping him: practical jokes, spoof phone calls, disguises, you name it, he did it!

WEAKNESSES

Despite Janice and Dr Septic's efforts, every so often, Hughie does lapse into his 'good old ways'. This is something which still gives them serious cause for concern, for fear that he might one day become a security risk. Especially as Janice knows that Hughie really is 'a good sort', just like his true father, the man who mysteriously 'disappeared' around the time Janice met Dr Septic.

SUPERHERO PROFILE

The Silver Ripple

FIRST HINT OF SUPERIORITY

The Silver Ripple is one of the most versatile, talented and courageous members of GOSH. His first inkling that he might be 'special' came when he was eleven. Having always been attracted to all things shiny, he was on his parents' front drive, giving their vintage Silver Streak V8 Roadster its weekly clean and polish, buffing the car's silver paintwork

until he could see his face in it. All of a sudden, he was seized with an urge to 'cuddle' the gleaming monster. So he did! And he felt what he later described as a 'huge bolt of electricity passing through my entire body, making me feel more alert and alive than I'd ever felt in my whole life and giving me the impression that, if I'd wanted to, I could have actually lifted the massive motor car high in the air with just one hand.'

But of course, that was a silly idea. And, more to the point, he still had the wheel trims and door handles to polish! So he got back to work and thought no more of it.

135

FIRST EVER SUPER-MISSION

Later that same day, his mum asked him to go to the local shops to get her some bread, butter and tin foil. He would have preferred not to. For his route to the shop took him through a part of town notorious for its roughness and the bad behaviour of its inhabitants (something rare in the Realms of Normality!). Nevertheless, being an obedient lad, he set off.

His journey to the shop passed without incident. However, on his way home he was confronted with the sort of thing he'd been dreading. A gang of about twenty thuggish-looking sixteen-year-olds were tormenting a

small boy, roughly pushing him and holding his toy high above his head and threatening to hurl it into a nearby pond. The poor child was sobbing uncontrollably and Alan's heart immediately went out to him. And naturally, he felt a huge surge of rage towards the yobs.

But what was he to do? He was very weedy, and definitely non-sporty. He was the studious type who spent his time reading, particularly books about science, as it was his ambition to become a doctor and help his fellow human beings. But he just couldn't ignore it. So he went up to the sneering, jeering yobs and said, 'You lot ought to be ashamed of

yourselves. You bunch of bullies! Give this poor little lad his toy back and leave him alone!' The biggest and ugliest yob said, 'What's it got to do with you, spekky-four-eyes?' then punched him so hard he dropped his shopping.

Doing his best not to cry, he bent down to pick it up and, as he did, the big thug kicked him hard on the backside, sending him sprawling. But then a strange thing happened. For the second time that day he felt that rush of electricity and vitality and power surge through his entire being, and he looked down to see that he was clutching the roll of tin foil. He was on his feet in a moment, and a

nano-second after that he was holding the astonished yob high above his head. Then, as easily as if he was throwing a tennis ball, he hurled the thug at his mates, flattening them like the pins at a bowling alley. After dumping the yobs in the pond, he reunited the little boy with his toy and took him home to his mum. Then, just as he was leaving, the little boy said, 'Wow! You were amazing! What a hero. And so silver!'

'What do you mean "silver"?' he asked.

'You went silver all over!' said the boy. 'While you were thrashing the yobs. And as you did, your muscles grew dead big and

rippled and glinted under your amazing silver body! You were just like one big silver ripple!'

DAY-TO-DAY IDENTITY

Dr Alan Noot.

SPECIAL POWERS

The Ripple can transform into any silver object. He's been a justice-dealing silver sword, a baddy-battering silver missile and a lethal silver boomerang.

PETS

The Ripple has a pond full of silver fish and a silver tabby cat called Hallmark.

ACHILLES HEEL

He's terrified of rust.

KERPOW!
THE ULTIMATE SUPERHERO'S HANDBOOK

SUPER-SIZING YOUR SUPERPOWERS!

'BioTensic TranZilliance'™
A BRIEF EXPLANATION

Except for people called David or Mary (and people who live in Burton-on-Trent), we all

possess something called 'bioTensic tranZilliance™. If you are able to access this inner super-force, taking on such horrors as One-Eyed Uber Trolls, Dripping Herberts and Rampant Spleen Chiggers will be a piece of cake (as will carrying really heavy shopping). Here is just one of many exercises which will enable you to connect with this most potent of inner super-powers.

EXERCISE 26
'WAFTING THE SQUIRREL'

Standing in front of a full-length mirror (or a shop window if you happen to be out and

about), put your hands behind your ears and push them forwards so that they stand out like those of an enraged bull elephant (or listless British monarch). Now, swaying slowly from side-to-side and rolling your eyes, open your mouth as wide as it will go and allow your tongue to flap about while intermittently uttering the words, 'Filbert, filbert, I'd really like a filbert!' Remember to keep your eyes fixed firmly on your reflection.

NB If at any time during this exercise you grin, giggle or guffaw, you will seriously damage, or even destroy your kinetic omnipotence cache, resulting in you being

plagued by harrowing night sweats and the permanent belief that you have turned into a wood pigeon.

After a while you will feel a small explosion in the region of your lower abdomen. This means that you a) have accessed your Kinetic Omnipotence Cache and can look forward to the imminent release of your `BioTensic tranZilliance™; b) need to get to the A and E Department of your local hospital really, really quickly; or c) have snapped the elastic on your undergarments.

Tip: if you're doing this in front of a shop window ignore any derisive comments or

144

jibes aimed at you by passers-by (or the small crowd of spectators who have gathered around you). Remember, you may one day become super, but they will always remain shallow and tedious.

SELF DEFENCE TECHNIQUES FOR SUPERHEROES
'FONG KWOK'

Please note! Fong Kwok is a non-contact self-defence system and should not be used simply for kicks! Remember, superheroes are commited to non-violence and only use force as a last resort. Irresponsible use of the following moves results in instant dismissal

from GOSH! and a place in the Superhero Hall of Shame. You have been warned!

1: THE TONGAN TROTTING DUCK FEINT (LEVEL 2)

'Never fails to leave opponents flabber-smacked!' DEXTER DOODLEBUG

2: THE PATAGONIAN WIGGLE (LEVEL 1)

'An absolute doddle! And so effective!' BODACIOUS BABE

3: REVERSE DOUBLE ELVIS WITH ATTENUATED BUTTERFLY SCOOP (LEVEL 10)

'I subdued an entire flock of Snowberian Crowbots using this astonishing technique'
THE SILVER RIPPLE

4: TRANSVERSE SIAMESE OCTOPUS SNATCH WITH DOUBLE BUTTOCK FLIP (LEVEL 6)

'Quite a tricky one this, but once I'd mastered it I was able to take on opponents fifteen times my size!' VEST AND PANTS LAD

MAINTAINING YOUR ANONYMITY

SOME TIPS

Please note: All twenty 'Maintaining your anonymity' tips are discussed in detail in Johnny Catbiscuit's international best-seller: *How to be Super!*

1) Avoid using superhero language in day-to-day situations. For instance, if Dr Alan Noot (the Silver Ripple) were to suddenly leap on to his desk and yell, '**ONE FALSE MOVE AND I'LL ZAP YOU FROM HERE TO ETERNITY!**' at a little old lady who had come to his surgery, it might raise a few eyebrows.

2) Resist the temptation to 'show off', e.g. don't suddenly transform in your local supermarket, then fly up and down the vegetable aisle yelling, **I'M SUPER! YOU LOT ARE JUST . . . ORDINARY! HA HA HA!** It's rude, arrogant and, most of all, very dangerous!

BONUS EXTRACT FROM *HOW TO BE SUPER!*
SUPERHERO IDENTITY THEFT

You must guard your superhero identity and associated licence, certificates and other documents very carefully, as there are many ordinary and extremely un-super people out there who are only too

149

keen to pretend to be you and take credit for all your brave deeds. For instance, in 2004 AS*, the Silver Ripple discovered that someone had been going around saying he was him and 'rescuing' hens from farmyards. However, the impostor turned out be a Dorset postman called Kevin Duddy, dressed in a silver survival blanket, fifty shiny crisp packets and some roasting foil, all of which his mother had adapted for him on her new digital sewing machine.

* *Anno Superfluous*

BONUS BONUS EXTRACT FROM *HOW TO BE SUPER!*
COPING WITH 'SPONTANEOUS REVERSION'

Spontaneous reversion is when, mid-rescue, you suddenly and unexpectedly change back from your super-self to your day-to-day self.

For example, having retro-jetted to Ancient Rome to rescue a very frightened little boy from an arena full of ravenous lions, bears and wolves, Time-Slip Sandra suddenly reverted from her six-foot-tall, statuesque, leather-and-bronze-clad super-self, to her somewhat less impressive,

151

day-to-day self – dental hygienist Kelly Dingle (5'2"). So, instead of hurling herself at the slavering beasts, super-suited and super-booted, and making short work of them with her lethal laser-sabre, she suddenly found herself wearing her everyday tunic and slacks and armed with nothing more than a glass of mouthwash and some dental floss. This had happened because the little boy had reminded her of her nephew, Steven, bringing back memories of a shared family holiday. Reminiscing about your humdrum existence whilst carrying out a rescue is just asking for trouble!

152

If you want to avoid spontaneous reversion, **DO NOT DO IT!** You have been warned!

For Sandra, it was a lesson well learned! Fortunately for her, her amazing transformation gave both the beasts and the Ancient Romans such a start that she was able to snatch the boy, re-revert and take him to a place of safety, then return to real-time unharmed. However, as Sandra later said to Johnny Catbiscuit, 'It was a close-run thing!'

EGMONT PRESS: ETHICAL PUBLISHING

Egmont Press is about turning writers into successful authors and children into passionate readers – producing books that enrich and entertain. As a responsible children's publisher, we go even further, considering the world in which our consumers are growing up.

Safety First
Naturally, all of our books meet legal safety requirements. But we go further than this; every book with play value is tested to the highest standards – if it fails, it's back to the drawing-board.

Made Fairly
We are working to ensure that the workers involved in our supply chain – the people that make our books – are treated with fairness and respect.

Responsible Forestry
We are committed to ensuring all our papers come from environmentally and socially responsible forest sources.

For more information, please visit our website at
www.egmont.co.uk/ethicalpublishing